Tony Blundell

OLIVER
and the Monsters

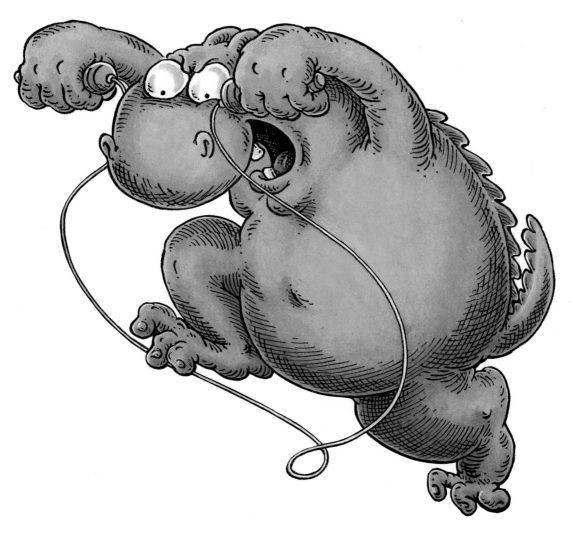

Gareth Stevens Publishing
MILWAUKEE

To Philippa, who was so patient,
and to Oliver, who wasn't

Library of Congress Cataloging-in-Publication Data

Blundell, Tony.
    Oliver and the monsters / by Tony Blundell.
       p. cm.
    Summary: Oliver hopes to keep monsters out of his bedroom at night by giving them a taste of their own medicine.
    ISBN 0-8368-1293-X
    [1. Monsters—Fiction. 2. Bedtime—Fiction. 3. Fear—Fiction. 4. Night—Fiction.] I. Title.
PZ7.B627201 1995
[E]—dc20
                                           94-23695

North American edition first published in 1995 by
Gareth Stevens Publishing
1555 North RiverCenter Drive, Suite 201
Milwaukee, Wisconsin 53212, USA

Original edition published in 1993 by Viking Children's Books Ltd. Text and illustrations © 1993 by Tony Blundell.

Printed in the United States of America

  3 4 5 6 7 8 9 99 98 97 96

It was the middle of the night,
but Oliver couldn't sleep.
Something was bothering him.

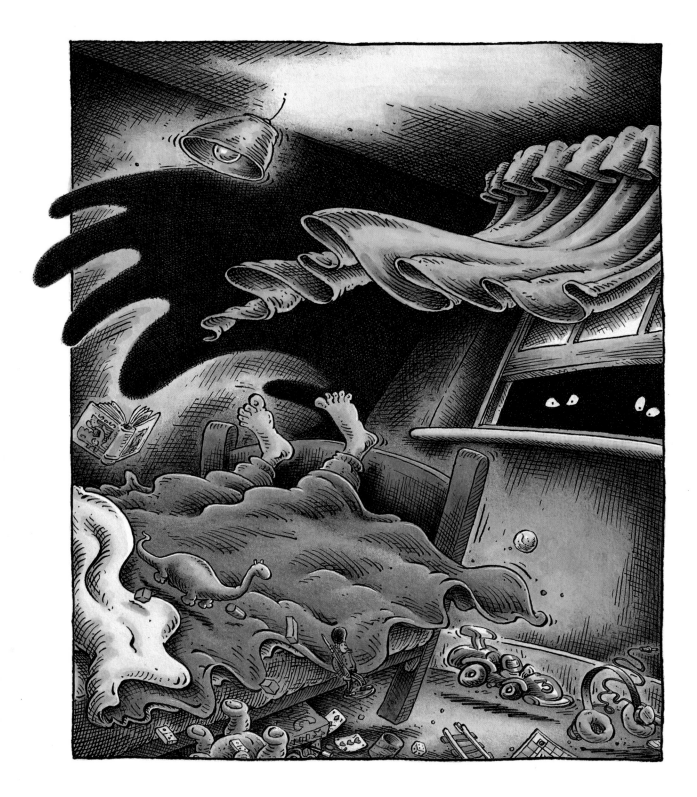

It wasn't the wind in the curtains . . .

or the shadowy shapes on the wall.

It was monsters — monsters — monsters!

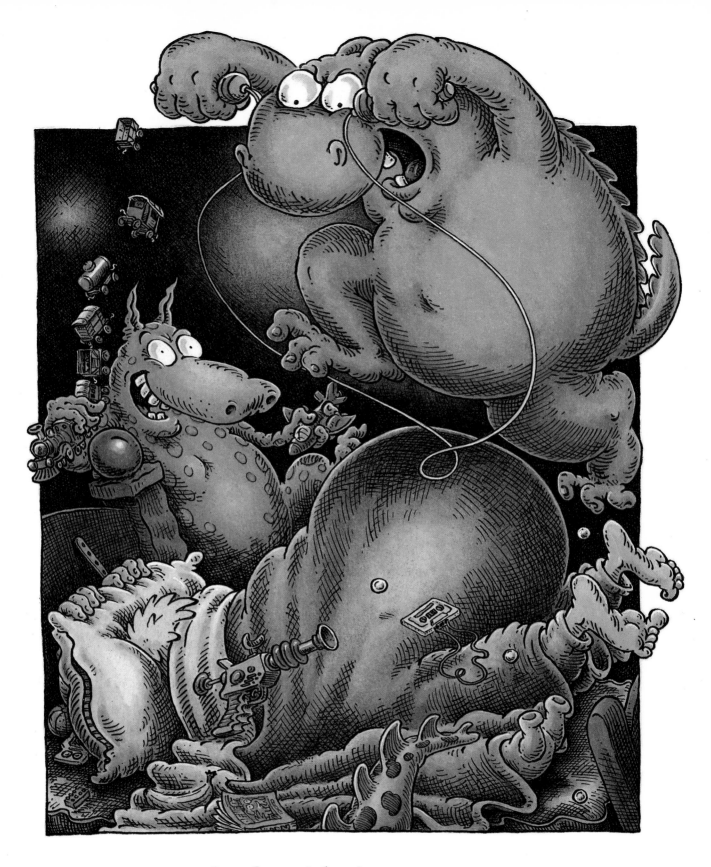

Night after night, it was monsters.

Oliver had had enough.
"Enough is enough!" he said.

He pulled on his shoes, picked up his flashlight,
and crept down the stairs . . .

9

across the garden . . .

and into the dark woods.

Soon the dark woods became a deep, dark forest . . .

and in the deepest, darkest part of the forest,
he found the house where the monsters lived.

Suddenly, Oliver wasn't scared at all.
He bounded up the gloomy staircase.

"All right, you monsters!" he said . . .

and burst into the monsters' bedroom.

"It's a ten-ton teddy!" cried the monsters,
leaping from their beds.

17

"And a colossal crocodile!" they shouted
as they tumbled down the stairs.

"And a rampaging rabbit!" they wailed, getting
stuck in the downstairs doorway.

"And a dastardly duck!" they squealed as
they burst into the room.

"And, OH NO, A BOY!" screamed the
leading monster. "STOP!!"

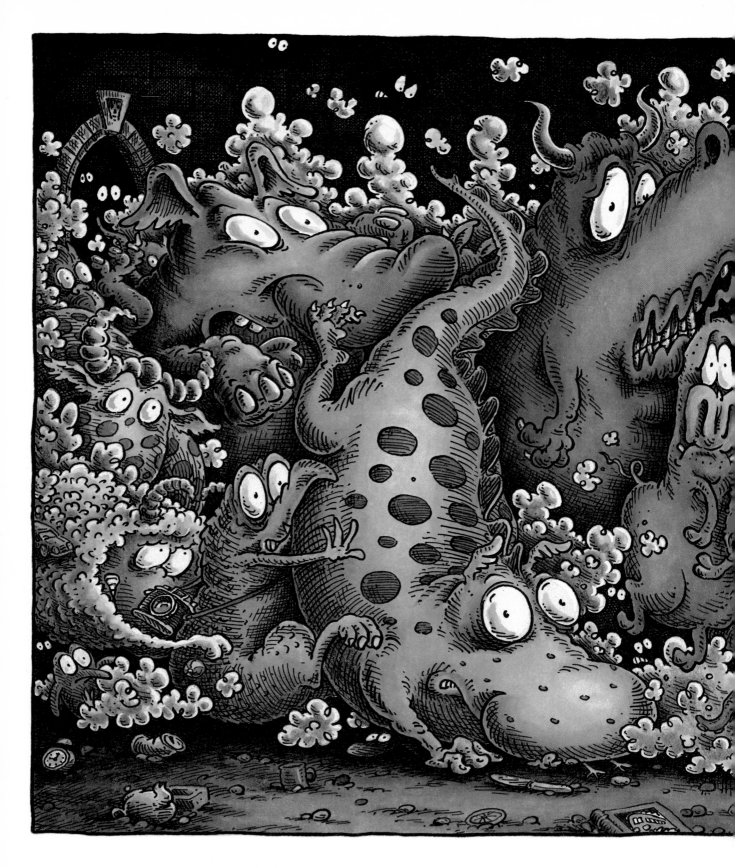

And the monsters did just that.

"Oh, you gave us such a fright," cried the
monsters as they picked themselves up.

23

"Well, now you know what it feels like,"
said Oliver. "After this, maybe you won't
bother me, night after night."

"Oh, we won't, we won't," agreed the monsters.

"Never again," they promised.

"As if we would," they added.

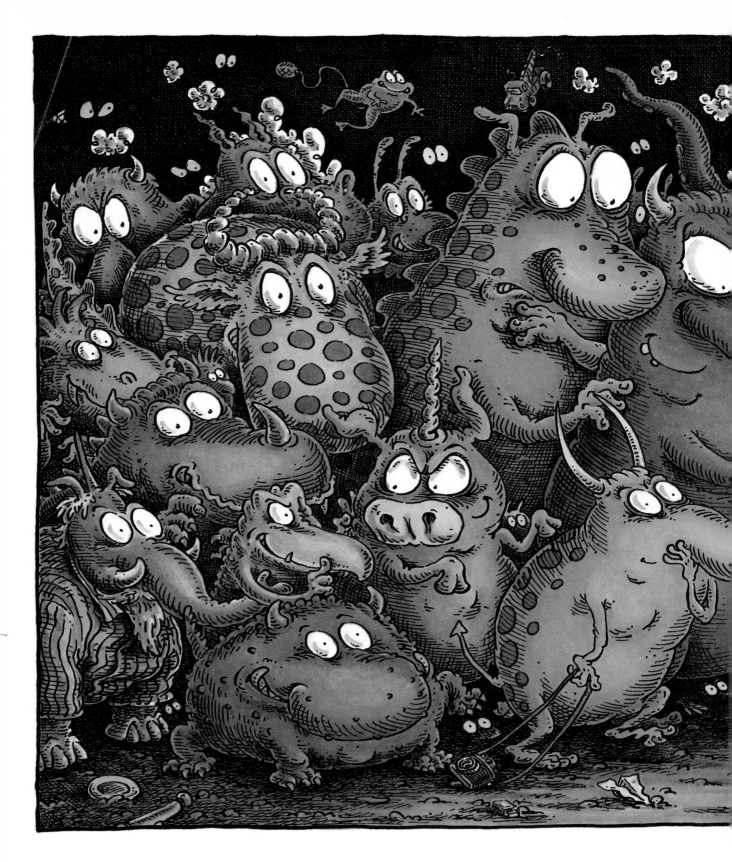

"Good," said Oliver. "Then I won't bother you!" And
they shook hands, claws, hoofs, and paws on the deal.

Oliver suddenly felt very tired.
"Time for bed," he said.

"We weren't *really* scared," called out the monsters.
"Boo!" shouted Oliver, and they all disappeared.

Soon, the deep, dark forest turned back into dark woods,
and the dark woods . . .

turned back into Oliver's bedroom.

"No more monsters," sighed Oliver
as his eyes began to close.

Of course, the monsters didn't keep their promise.
Monsters never do!